LITTLE WHITE DOGS

CAN'T JUMP

BRUCE WHATLEY • ROSIE SMITH

To Smudge, our new best friend

Angus&Robertson
An imprint of HarperCollins*Publishers*, Australia

First published in Australia in 2001
by HarperCollins*Publishers* Pty Limited
ABN 36 009 913 517
A member of the HarperCollins*Publishers* (Australia) Pty Limited Group
http://www. harpercollins.com.au

HarperCollins*Publishers*
25 Ryde Road, Pymble, Sydney, NSW 2073, Australia
31 View Road, Glenfield, Auckland 10, New Zealand
77–85 Fulham Palace Road, London W6 8JB, United Kingdom
Hazelton Lanes, 55 Avenue Road, Suite 2900, Toronto, Ontario M5R 3L2
and 1995 Markham Road, Scarborough, Ontario M1B 5M8, Canada
10 East 53rd Street, New York NY 10022, USA

National Library of Australia Cataloguing-in-Publication data:

Whatley, Bruce.
Little white dogs can't jump.
ISBN 0 207 19875 6 (hbk)
ISBN 0 207 19883 7 (pbk)
1. Dogs - Juvenile fiction. I. Smith, Rosie, 1956- . II. Title.
A823.3

Printed in China by Everbest Printing Co. Ltd on 128gsm matt art.

5 4 3 2 1   01 02 03 04

LITTLE WHITE DOGS
CAN'T JUMP

BRUCE WHATLEY • ROSIE SMITH

Angus&Robertson
An imprint of HarperCollinsPublishers

My dog, Smudge,
has got really short legs.
Which makes it very difficult
for him to jump.

Especially up into
the back of the car.

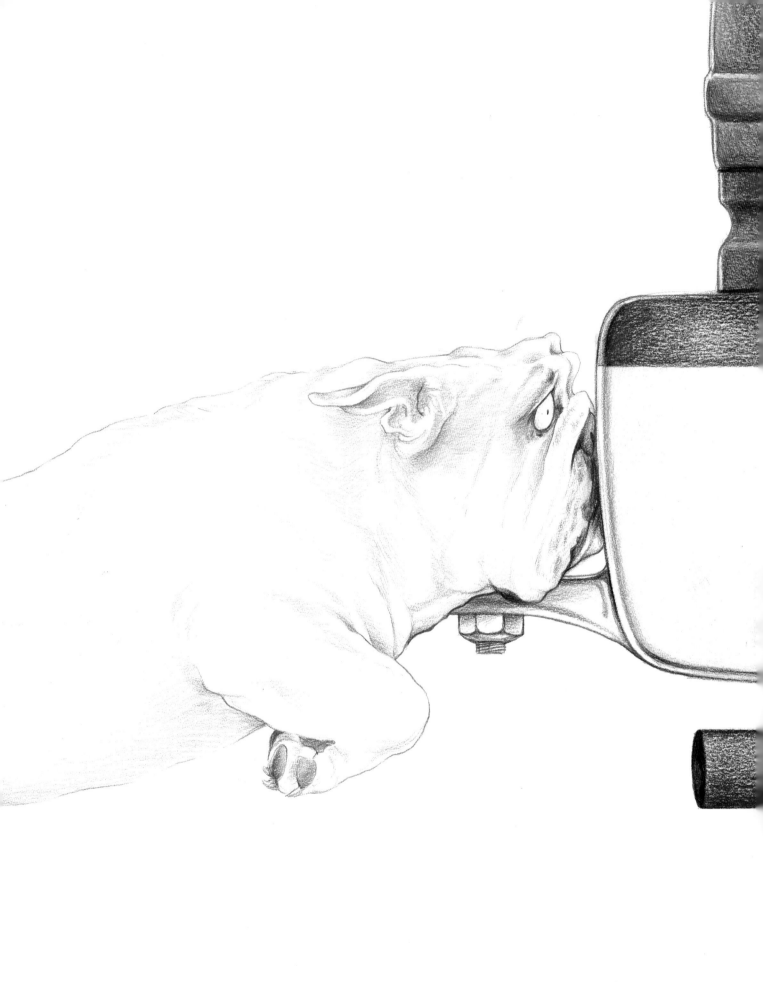

So I tried dressing him up
as a famous basketball player
to make him feel taller.
And gave him something to jump at.

But I don't think little
white dogs can jump.

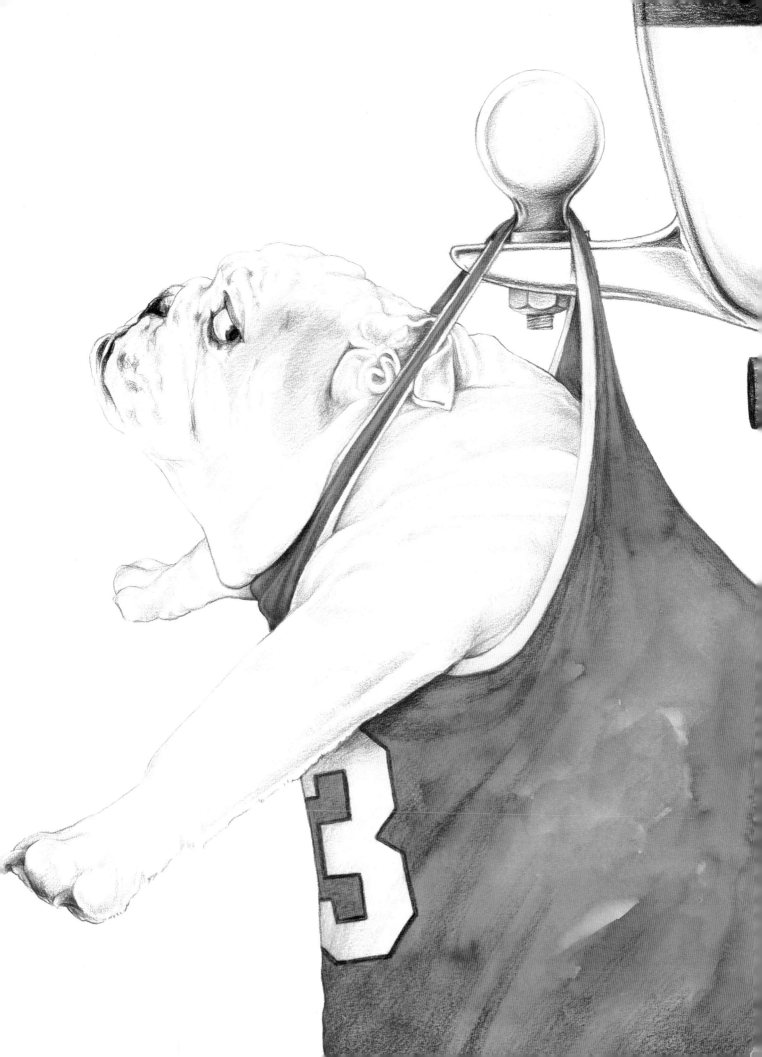

Smudge needed some help.
I got some strong springs, rope
and wood and made a Smudgematic
dog-lifter that has a little platform
for Smudge to stand on.
And a red button that says 'up'.

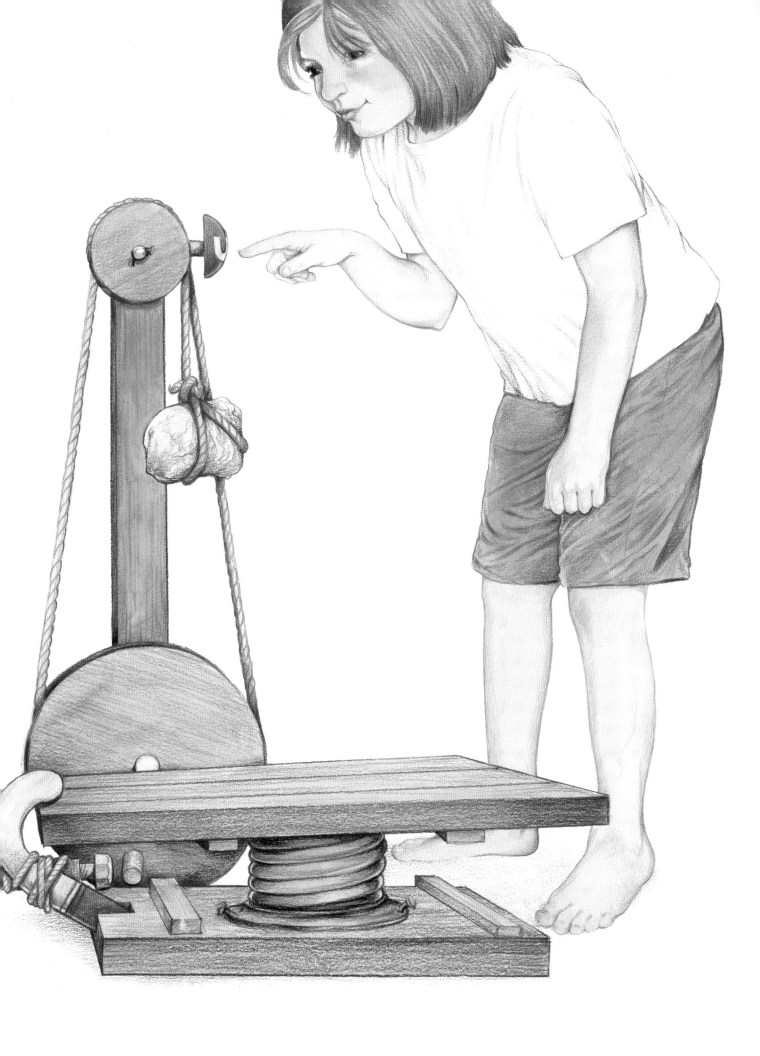

I guess the springs were
a little too strong!

Now Smudge can't jump
and is afraid of small spaces.

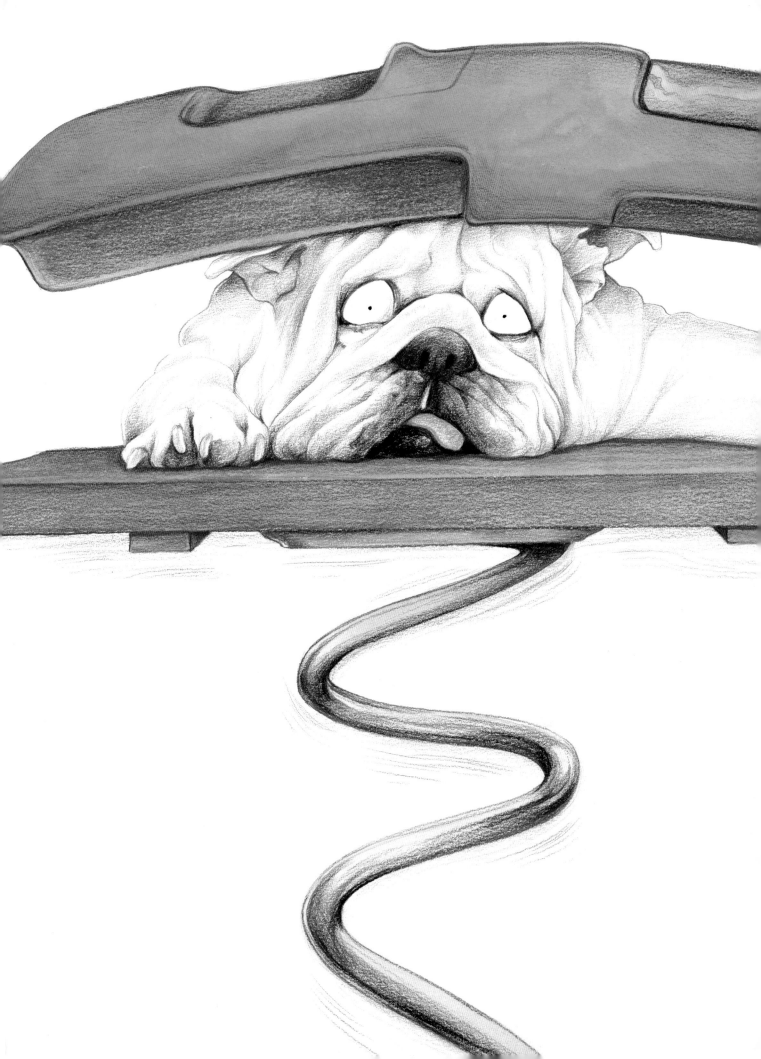

I borrowed my brother's skateboard
and made a ramp with the wood
from the Smudgematic dog-lifter.

Then I took Smudge to the top
of our drive.

And let him go.

Now Smudge can't jump,
is afraid of small spaces
and hates heights.

I remembered borrowing a book
from the library about a man in
a circus who shot out of cannons.

This seemed like a good idea.

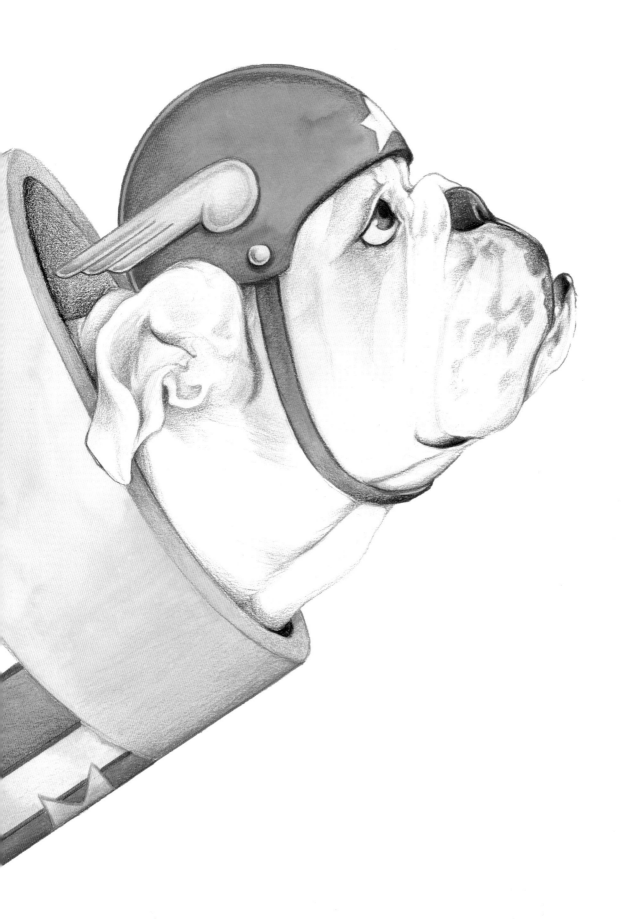

Smudge didn't think so.

Now he can't jump,
is afraid of small spaces,
hates heights and
is scared of loud noises.

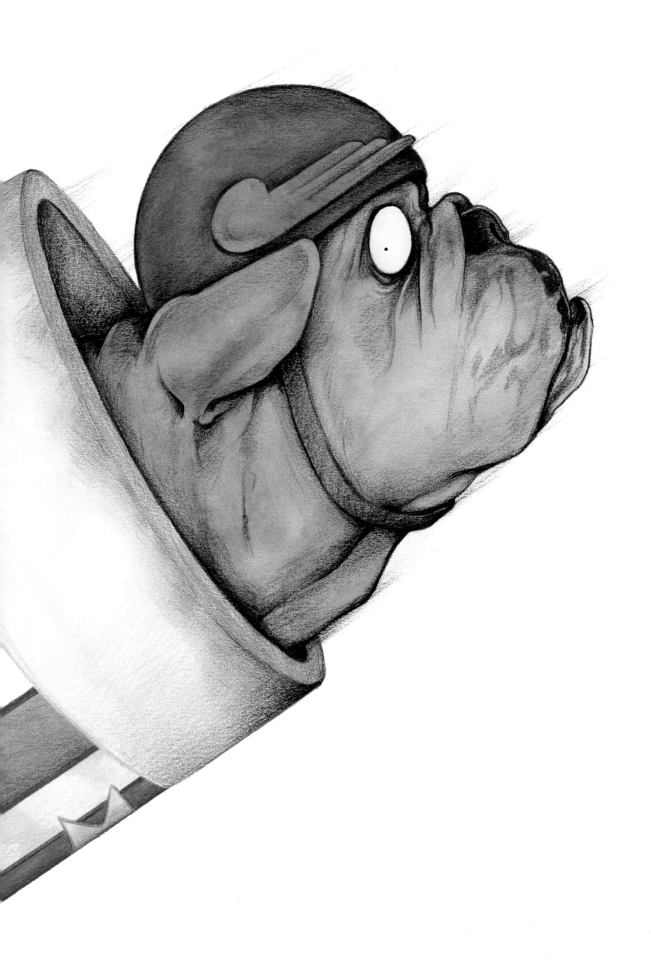

One of my favourite cartoon characters used a catapult to fling himself after a really fast bird. This seemed like a good idea. I could catapult Smudge into the back of the car.

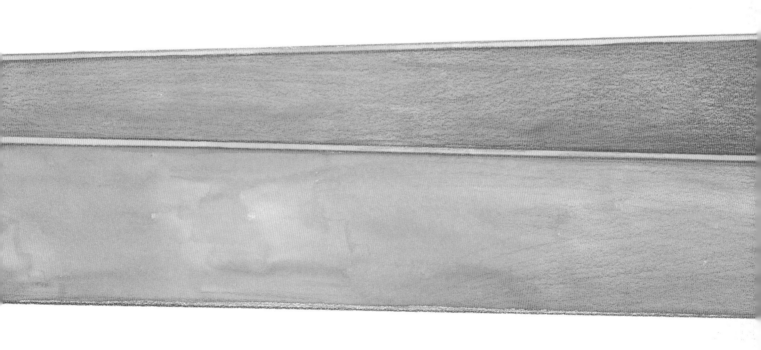

Or maybe the front of the car!

Now Smudge can't jump,
is afraid of small spaces, hates heights,
is scared of loud noises and
moving at great speed.

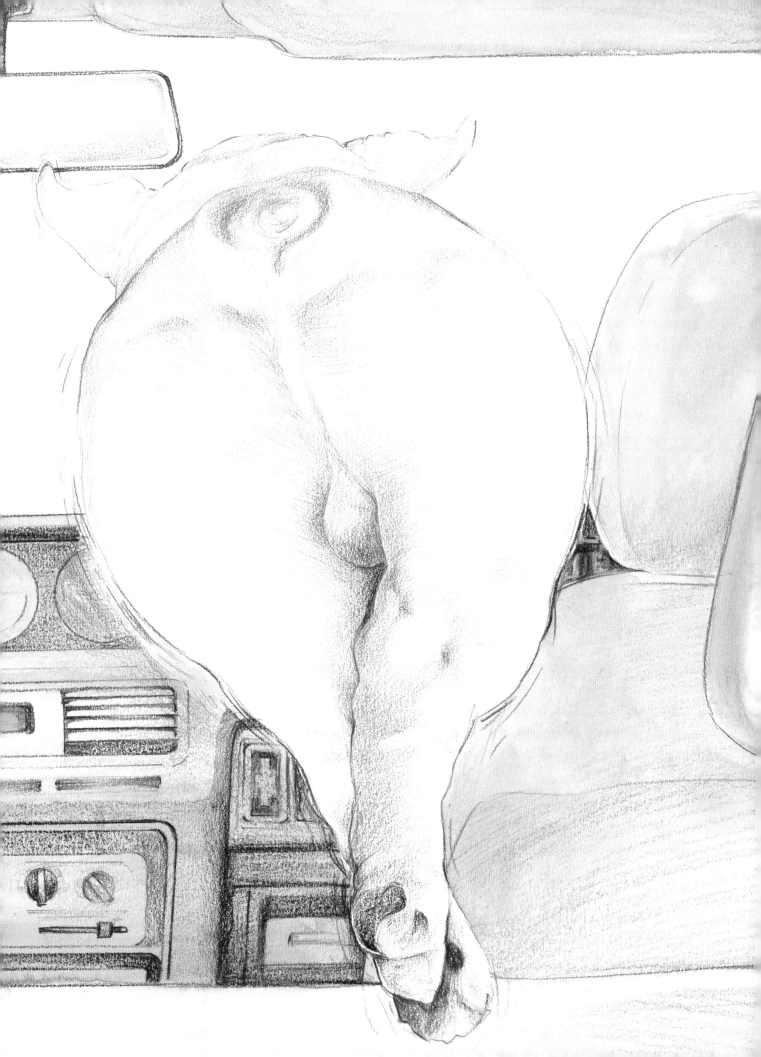

It was time for all the family
to put their heads together and find
a way to get Smudge up into the car.

Mum had an idea.

We'd get another car.
One just the right height for Smudge.

Mum thought this was a really
good idea.

So did Smudge.

Especially as little white
dogs can't jump.

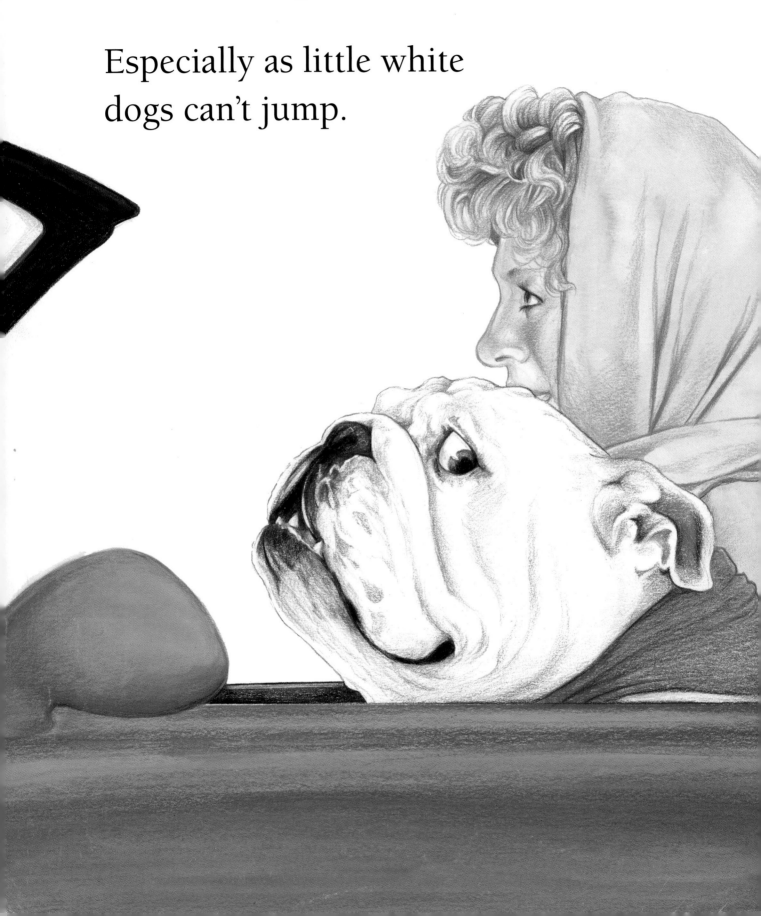